TATTLE
TAILS

Read all the books about Barkley's School for Dogs!

Coming Soon!

TATTLE TAILS

By Marcia Thornton Jones and Debbie Dadey

Illustrated by Amy Wummer

Hyperion Books for Children
New York

To Mariel, Ian, and Julia Abbene, great neighbors   —DD

To Ed Amend, Lee Bamberger, Judy Minnehan, and Lewanna Sexton—four dog-awesome friends!
                                                                          —MTJ

Printed in the United States of America
First Edition
1 3 5 7 9 10 8 6 4 2
Book design by Dawn Adelman
This book is set in 14-pt. Cheltenham.
ISBN 0-7868-1678-3
Visit www.barkleyschool.com

Contents

SMALL DOG, BIG MOUTH

"News! News! I have news!" Harry hopped in front of me when I arrived at the Barkley's School for Dogs play yard.

Harry, a Westie, may be one of the smaller dogs at Barkley's, but he definitely doesn't have the smallest mouth. It's a Fido Fact that Harry likes to talk. Lately he'd been spreading news about every pup in the yard faster than a jumping tick.

I smiled down at my little friend. His ears stood straight up, and his wiry tail

1

waved like a flag on his rear end. His pink tongue licked at his white beard. He hopped up and down, he was so excited.

"What is it this time?" I asked.

Usually, Harry's chatter didn't bother me. After all, I consider myself something of a Wonder Dog, and Wonder Dogs do not let a little gossip bother them. Besides, Harry's news wasn't always tail-thumping thrilling. I sat down to listen.

"Did you hear about Petey?" Harry asked.

I shook my head and glanced across the yard. Petey, a little brown-and-white fellow, was snooping around a soft mound of dirt.

"Fred caught him digging holes," Harry said.

I scratched at a flea. Fred, the owner of Barkley's School for Dogs, was bound to be a little unhappy, but Petey always dug holes, so that was nothing new. I had a feeling I knew how Petey got caught, though. "Did you tell on Petey?" I asked.

Harry ignored my question. "Rhett and Scarlett got into a growling match, did you know that?" Harry asked. "Scarlett found out that Rhett was playing chase with Blondie. Scarlett didn't like it one bit."

I yawned. The two Irish setters sometimes got a little growly, but they always sniffed noses and made up. "How did

Scarlett find out?" I asked, even though I already knew the answer.

Harry pretended he didn't hear me, but those perky ears hadn't missed my question. "Guess what?" Harry said in a hushed tone. "Bubba spilled a bag of kibble in the front office! I showed Fred the mess, and he gave me a treat."

I circled three times and plopped down on the ground for a nap. After all, Bubba was just a pup and everyone knew that pups tended to make messes sometimes.

Harry wasn't finished. He jumped up and down. "There's something else," my little friend yipped. "You'll never believe it!"

Harry waited for me to ask for the details. I kept my mouth shut. Finally, he spilled the information.

"It's about Blondie," Harry said, a little grin curling the ends of his mouth.

My ears twitched. Blondie was one of

my best friends and just about the pretti-
est dog in the neighborhood. I didn't like
the fact that Harry was talking about her
one bit.

"She lied!" Harry yipped.

I felt a growl working its way up from
my chest. I knew Blondie, and I knew she
was no liar. Harry had to be wrong, but
getting upset about it wasn't going to do
any good. I swallowed my growl and
looked at Harry. "What's gotten into you?

You shouldn't spread rumors like that," I told him. "It isn't nice. One of these days you're going to end up in big trouble because of telling stories."

Harry looked up at me with his huge brown eyes. "It's no lie," he assured me. "Let me tell you all about it."

I shook my head. "I'm not going to listen to any more big tales from a tattletale like you."

"How dare you call me a tattletale!" he snapped. Then, Harry snarled at me!

SNiTCH

I watched Harry's wiry tail march across the yard. I didn't like the way he looked over his shoulder and stuck out his tongue. I was going to follow, but just then Floyd walked up.

Floyd's a beagle and one of the best friends a hound could ever hope for. Usually, he carried something to chew on. Today was no different. A brown shoe dangled from his jaws. I thought I had seen that shoe before, but I was worried about something else.

"What's up with Harry?" I asked Floyd. "He's acting like a cat gnawed his tail. That's not like him. He's usually such a happy hound."

"Harry's humans got a new puppy and then they went on vacation," Floyd whispered. I had to listen hard, since his mouth was full of shoe. "They took the puppy with them, but they didn't take Harry. Harry's humans are making him spend the entire week right here at Barkley's School for Dogs. Even the nights!"

I shuddered. Being at Barkley's during the day was one thing, but staying all night was asking for disaster. And disaster was spelled S-W-E-E-T-C-A-K-E-S.

Sweetcakes belonged to Fred Barkley, and she lived at Barkley's School for Dogs. Besides being the meanest dog this side of the moon, it was the dog-honest truth that she did not like anyone else

10

sharing Fred. Of course, the worst part of Harry's situation was being away from his humans. I couldn't imagine my human leaving me behind for a whole week.

"No wonder Harry is so grumpy," I said. "That's not fair."

Floyd nodded, and drool dripped onto the shoe. "Life with puppies is no picnic. They chew your ears and always want attention. I'm sure that's why the puppy went and Harry stayed. His humans could only take one dog on vacation."

I scratched my left ear and nodded. Once, a whole litter of puppies jumped on me. I knew how much puppy teeth hurt. I truly felt sorry for Harry.

That changed in ten seconds flat when Harry appeared beside Floyd and me. Harry barked as though the mailman were coming. "Here! Here! Here!"

"What's wrong?" I asked Harry.

Harry didn't answer, he just kept barking, "Here! Here! Here!"

"Come on Harry," I said softly. "Stop all that noise and tell me what's wrong."

But Harry didn't stop. In fact, he barked even louder, until Fred Barkley showed up beside him.

Fred took one look at Floyd. "What are you doing?" Fred asked, snatching the shoe from Floyd's mouth. Slobber dribbled out of the shoe, and small teeth marks covered the toe.

Floyd whimpered he was sorry, but

Fred was too upset to listen. He grabbed Floyd's collar and led him to the dreaded time-out area, but not before petting Harry right between his ears. "Good dog," Fred said.

Harry's tail sped up, and he licked Fred's hand.

"Why did you do that?" I snapped at Harry once Fred walked away. "Floyd has never been in time-out his entire life."

"I knew Fred would not be happy about Floyd chewing on his shoes," Harry said, as if that explained everything.

I looked at Harry. Thanks to him, Floyd had earned his first time-out. I must say, I lost my temper. I did something I never should have done.

I growled.

If there was one thing Fred did not allow, it was fighting. Fred turned and pointed a single finger at me. He said the two most dreaded words known to any dog, big or small.

"Bad dog!"

TATTLETALE

Time-out. I knew all about it, and that's right where I was headed. Fred marched me toward the back of the yard.

Sweetcakes, Barkley's very own bully, and her sidekick, Clyde, snickered as I was led past.

I know most Doberman pinschers are nice, but Sweetcakes is not like most Dobermans. In fact, Sweetcakes is not like most dogs. She's more like a monster from outer space. "There goes Jack, the Underwear Dog," Sweetcakes said.

"Yeah. Yeah. Underwear," Clyde the bulldog repeated.

"That's WONDER Dog," I started to bark, but Fred put a hand on my head, and I swallowed my words.

Fred led me around the shed and hooked me to a leash beside Floyd. Then he left us all alone. That's the worst part of time-out. No dog likes being alone. Fortunately for me, I had good friends. Friends like Blondie.

Blondie waited until Fred was out of sight, then she sneaked back to keep us company. Usually, just seeing Blondie's halo of white poodle curls and her big brown eyes made my tail wag. But today, something was wrong. Blondie wasn't smiling. In fact, she looked a little mad.

"It's not like you to be mean, Jack," Blondie said.

"Mean? Me?" I whimpered. "What did I do?"

"And right when Harry needs his friends the most," Blondie added, as if I hadn't said a word.

"It was Harry's fault," I told Blondie. "He got Floyd and me in trouble."

"Don't you understand?" Blondie asked. "Harry is sad that his humans left him behind, and what do you do? You growl at him and call him a tattletale. There are some things real friends would never do."

"Yeah," I told her. "Real friends wouldn't tattle."

"Oh, Jack," Blondie said as she turned to leave. "Think what would have happened if Floyd had destroyed Fred's favorite shoes? Sometimes, telling is important."

Floyd bowed his head, and his ears dragged on the ground. "I didn't mean to chew Fred's shoe," he said. "I grabbed the first thing in sight when I lost my tennis

ball. I'm glad Harry stopped me, or else I'd be in bigger trouble."

Blondie smiled at Floyd. She looked at me, and her smile faded. "We all need to be a little nicer until Harry's family returns." And then, Blondie walked away from me.

I couldn't believe it. I had ended up in time-out, but Blondie didn't care. Things were bad, very bad; but suddenly, they got even worse.

DING

"Hey, Under Dog," said a voice. I knew that voice and it was trouble.

"That's *Wonder* Dog," I said, looking up at the tall brick wall surrounding Barkley's School for Dogs. Sure enough, sitting on top of the wall was a cat, the neighborhood pest. Her owner, Miss Frimple, named her Razzmatazz, but everyone called her Tazz. If you ask me, they should have called her Pain in the Rump.

"You look a bit misUNDERstood to me,"

Tazz purred. "Wouldn't that make you Under Dog instead of a Wonder Dog?"

I groaned. Being a Wonder Dog certainly did make life complicated. I tried to make the world a better place, and look where it had gotten me. "Not now, Tazz," I said with a whine. "I am in no mood to be teased."

I felt like eating Tazz's furry tail for a snack, but there was no way to reach her. Floyd sighed and put his paws over his eyes, pretending he didn't see or hear a thing.

Tazz licked a paw and used it to smooth her long whiskers. "You're not mad at me, are you?" she purred. "After all, we're friends."

"Friends!" I snapped. "Friends don't make fun of each other when they're in a bad mood."

"Hey," Floyd said. "Isn't that what Blondie told you about Harry?"

I sat down on my tail. I thought long and hard for at least five seconds. That's when a bell went off inside my head. *Ding!* Tazz was trying to teach me a lesson. "Thanks, Tazz," I said quietly.

Tazz looked at me and swished her tail. I thought I saw something like a grin on her face. "I guess you aren't such silly dogs after all."

"Gee," Floyd said with a bashful grin. "Thanks!"

Tazz was right. I am a smart dog. A

Wonder Dog, in fact. I made up my mind right then and there to apologize to Harry for calling him a tattletale. It looked like I wouldn't have to wait, because Harry trotted around the corner.

"Harry," I said, "I have something to say to you."

Harry didn't pay any attention to me. Instead, he eyed Tazz on the wall. "That's a CAT!" Harry said. "Jack is talking to a CAT!"

"Now, wait a minute," Floyd said. "Tazz is no ordinary cat."

"Of course not," Tazz interrupted. "I'm extraordinary."

"I'm telling," Harry said. "You shouldn't be playing with a cat while in time-out."

Tazz stood up and stretched, showing every one of her sharp claws. "Cats can do whatever they want," she purred. "But even if Jack shouldn't have been talking to me, why would you want to tell on your friend?"

Harry smacked his lips and blinked his eyes. "Because cats stir up trouble. Fred will be very glad when he realizes I stopped trouble before it even happened."

"Trouble?" Tazz said. "I was just enjoying the sun. There's no trouble here. Unless, of course, you choose to make a little trouble."

"I won't get in trouble because of a cat," Harry said. "I'm going to do something."

"What are you going to do?" Floyd asked with a whimper.

I didn't have to ask. I knew exactly what Harry planned. I was right.

"CAT! CAT! CAT!" Harry barked. "CAT! CAT! CAT!"

In less than seventeen seconds, twenty dogs came skidding around the corner of the shed. They weren't alone. Fred was with them, and he didn't look happy.

LESSONS

"What's all the fuss?" Fred asked.

Harry barked, his two feet stretched up the wall and his nose pointed straight at the furry cat. Twenty other dogs barked and jumped, trying to reach Tazz. Floyd and I just sat, shaking our heads.

Fred must have felt the same way. He leaned over to Harry and looked the little rascal right in the eyes. "Harry, stop barking," Fred said sharply. "It's only a cat."

"Hmph," Tazz nearly hissed. "I'm not just *any* cat." With that, she hopped off the other side of the wall and out of sight. Without a fuzzy cat tail swishing just out of muzzle's reach, the other dogs lost interest and wandered off, too.

"That cat wasn't hurting anyone," Fred told Harry.

Harry's barking stopped with a questioning whine. Then he wagged his flag of a tail and made a little yip.

This time, Fred did not pet Harry between the ears. Instead, he put a finger on Harry's nose. "Shhh. No barking," Fred said in a very stern voice.

Harry was expecting to get his head scratched. He put his tail between his legs and sulked away. I had to admit I felt a little sorry for him, but it's a Fido Fact that Harry had brought it on himself.

I forgot about Harry when Fred unhooked Floyd and me from time-out. "Okay, let's see what we can learn today," Fred said giving me a pat on the head.

Fred had this silly idea that we had to learn things at school, so every day he tried to teach us tricks. I had to admit, running through tunnels wasn't bad, but today Fred had something else in mind.

"Today, we'll work on self-control," Fred announced to all the dogs, and then looked right at me. "Some of us need extra practice in that area."

Self-control? A Wonder Dog is a master of control. This lesson would be a snap for me.

As always, Sweetcakes went first. If any other dog dared dart in front of her, Sweetcakes would growl and bat the poor pooch out of the way. It bothered me that Fred always let his dog go first, but that's the way it was and there was no use worrying about it. At least it gave the rest of us a chance to see what Fred expected us to do.

I stared in disbelief as Sweetcakes did the trick. Surely this was a mistake. It couldn't be true. I mean, a lot of Fred's ideas are silly. Ideas like jumping over bars and walking across a teeter-totter when a dog knows good and well that it's much faster to zip under them. But this time, his idea was downright crazy, and that's the dog-honest truth.

Sweetcakes sat like a queen as Fred put

a cookie on her long dark snout. Fred waved his hand. Sweetcakes walked five feet away, turned around, and walked back to Fred. The entire time the cookie sat perched on Sweetcakes's nose.

I shook my head. What kind of crazy dog would carry a cookie on her nose? Any self-respecting Wonder Dog would eat that treat in no time flat. After all, what was the point of getting crumbs on top of a dog's nose?

Fred finally lowered his hand, and

Sweetcakes tilted her head. The cookie fell. Sweetcakes caught the treat and gobbled it up in one bite. Sweetcakes grinned at the rest of us. "Now you know how it's done," she said.

"That's the silliest thing I ever saw," I told Woodrow. "Everyone knows there are easier ways to eat a cookie. Besides, it's not polite to play with food."

Woodrow, the smartest old bassett hound around, nodded. "But it's what

Fred wants us to do," he said. "I guess I'll give it a try." Woodrow held that treat on his nose for a full ten seconds before it slipped.

"Very good job," Fred said, patting Woodrow on the head and rewarding him with the cookie.

All the dogs gave it a try, until finally Fred looked at me.

I sat, my mouth hanging open in disbelief. Had Fred lost his human mind? At home, Maggie, the most perfect human in the world, got sent to her room for playing with food. Now Fred expected us all to play with cookies as if they were juggling balls. Obviously, it was up to a Wonder Dog to save the day before Fred got in trouble like Maggie did.

"Okay, Jack," Fred said. "Let's see if you can do this."

I grinned. I would show Fred once and for all that I had Wonder Dog manners.

I sat like a king while Fred put the cookie on my nose. It smelled like peanut butter. Then, before a crumb had time to settle in my silky hair, I tilted my head and gobbled up that treat before Fred had a chance to blink his eyes.

"No, Jack," Fred said. "Try again." He pulled out another cookie. My eyes crossed as Fred balanced the treat on my nose. *Gulp.* That cookie was gone faster than snow on a July day. I grinned up at

Fred, waiting for him to scratch my ears because I was the only dog that didn't play with his food. My manners were dog-perfect.

Instead, Fred shook his head and sighed. Human faces are hard to understand. After all, they never growl, and their ears don't move one bit. Still, I knew the look on Fred's face. Fred was not happy, and it was because of me. I felt my tail droop, and I whimpered.

Fred, being human, did not understand me. "We'll try again later," he said. Then he set the box of cookies down and turned his attention to Bubba, the little pup full of wiggles and wags. Bubba had found a piece of rope in the yard. And now Fred was playing tug-of-war to get it loose.

I didn't feel like playing. I had to figure out what went wrong. I had shown Fred the proper way to eat a cookie, hadn't I?

As I sat thinking, my Wonder Dog nose caught a whiff of something—something that made my nose twitch and my tongue drop out of my mouth. Cookies! The box of cookies was only two steps away.

Some things a dog just cannot help. Things like wagging his tail, scratching at fleas, and flopping his hind leg during a good belly rub. That's why no one should blame me for what I did next.

COOKIE THIEF

I took two giant steps, and the cookie box was in my Wonder Dog jaws. With a quick shake, a pile of delicious cookies spilled to the ground. On my third bite, something interrupted my feast.

Harry.

"Look! Look!" Harry yapped to Fred. "Look at Jack!"

Fortunately, Fred was busy pulling with all his might in a ferocious game of tug-of-war with Bubba.

"Shh," I tried to warn Harry. Have you

ever tried to talk with a mouth full of cookies? Let me tell you, it isn't exactly pretty. Cookie crumbs flew everywhere.

"LOOK! LOOK!" Harry barked even louder. "Jack is a cookie thief."

Fred, still tugging on his end of the rope, didn't even turn around. "Hush, Harry," he called over his shoulder. "No more barking."

I swallowed a cookie whole. "Look," I told Harry. "Fred doesn't want to be

bothered, and there is no need to start your tattle-telling. I'll share the treats with you."

Harry stopped barking long enough to give me a sneer. "I prefer to get my cookies the honest way, and I'm sure Fred will be happy that I do, too." Then Harry pointed his big black nose up in the air and let loose with a long howl. "LOOOOOOOOK!"

Every set of eyes, including Fred's, turned to do exactly what Harry wanted them to. They looked.

Fred dropped his end of the rope, making Bubba extremely happy, and marched across the yard to where I sat. I looked up and wrinkled my forehead, hoping for the best.

"Jack, what am I going to do with you?" Fred asked. He leaned over and snatched what was left of the cookies off the ground.

I tilted my head and wagged my tail. I had plenty of ideas about what we could do. We could go for a walk in the park or toss a tennis ball around. Heck, I would even settle for a good tummy rub. What did Fred do? He took his box of cookies and went inside.

"Stop," Harry yipped. "I want a cookie! I deserve a cookie." Fred did not come back outside.

"This is all your fault," Harry yipped.

"My fault?" I nearly howled. "You're the one who tattled to Fred. If you'd kept your snout shut, Fred never would've known, and we both could be munching cookies to our tummies' content. Besides, friends aren't supposed to tattle on each other."

"Friends? What do you know about being friends?" Harry's voice ended in a snarl. Then he turned away and stalked across the yard.

I wasn't sure what Harry meant by that,

but I was too tired to find out. All those treats had made me pretty sleepy. A nap was just what I needed. I twirled around three times and snuggled into a ball. Of course, it was not to be.

"That's not true," I overheard Floyd saying to Harry. My nose suddenly got dry, and I knew Harry had been saying bad things about me. A Wonder Dog just knows these types of things. My ears perked up a good two inches.

Floyd and Harry were over by the wall, but Floyd looked at me before telling Harry, "You'd better watch what you say."

Harry's little tail wagged faster than his tongue. "But it's true," he barked.

Floyd shook his head and chomped down hard on a rubber ball. I decided it was time to see what was happening. I walked over to the wall, but Harry was obviously not happy to see me. "Well," he yipped, "if it isn't the cookie thief."

Before I even had a chance to sniff,
Harry turned his tail on me and pranced
away.

Floyd didn't say a word. Blondie, how-
ever, had a thing or two to say. "I can't
believe it!" Blondie snapped at me when
she walked by.

I looked at her and nodded. "I know. It's
hard to believe a little dog like that could
tell so many big tales on a friend."

"No," Blondie said. "It's hard to believe

you haven't apologized to Harry for calling him a tattletale. No wonder he's upset."

It bothered me more than a little that I kept getting into trouble because of Harry's tattling. Why did Blondie expect me to be the first to say I was sorry? That's exactly what I asked her.

"Jack," Blondie said, locking her big brown eyes on my own. "More than anything, Harry needs us right now. Just

think how terrible he must feel knowing a little squirt of a pup is romping with his family while poor Harry has to stay here. With Sweetcakes."

I did what Blondie said and tried to imagine it. Suddenly, my tail sagged. My ears drooped. I felt sad and lonely, too. More than anything, I longed for a scratch between my ears from my human, Maggie.

Blondie nudged my shoulder. "See? Harry's not a bad dog," she said. "He's only sad and needs a little extra attention. Besides, it's bad enough that he misses his humans, now he thinks you're not his friend, too. More than anything, Harry needs his friends right now."

Blondie had a point. I had hurt Harry's feelings. I needed to apologize. I just didn't know how hard that would be.

FORGIVE AND FORGET

I tried. Really I did, but Harry is one hard pup to catch. He didn't help my mood much either, come to think about it. Harry went from dog to dog, tattling to every hound about me.

By the time I found Harry, he was already talking to Rhett and Scarlett. "Jack likes cats better than dogs," Harry said.

"I do not," I interrupted, but Rhett and Scarlett didn't bother listening to me. "Cat lover" is just about the worst thing

you can call a dog. The two Irish setters
pointed their slender noses high in the
air and trotted away.

Next, Harry found Casanova. "Watch
out for Jack," Harry told the little
Chihuahua. "He calls his friends names
and doesn't believe what they say."

"I believe my friends," I argued, but it
was too late. Harry turned his back on me
and his pointy tail trotted away.

I tried to stop Harry from saying

anything else, but he was too fast for me. "It's Jack's fault we didn't get more cookies," Harry told Floyd. "Jack ate cookies when he wasn't supposed to, so Fred put them away for good. I bet we never ever get another cookie, and it's all Jack's fault."

"Don't believe him," I told Floyd, but I could tell by Floyd's eyes that he wondered if Harry could be right.

I trotted behind Harry, trying to stop him from tattling to the other dogs about

my mistakes. "I'm sorry I got mad this morning," I whined. "Really, I am."

Harry never looked back at me. Soon, all the dogs at Barkley's held their noses up in the air when I came by. Instead of apologizing to Harry, I wanted to feed him to Sweetcakes as an afternoon snack.

"I have had it with that tattling tail," I said, finally sitting down next to Woodrow. At least Woodrow wasn't mad at me. "Maybe friendship isn't worth all this trouble," I said.

Woodrow nestled in his favorite nap-ping spot. Bubba the pup was curled nearby. "Friends are always worth more than a little trouble. Though I agree, Harry does like to tell on other dogs," Woodrow said with a yawn.

"I think tattling is the worst thing a dog can do," I said with a whine. "Why are you still talking to me? After all, Harry is con-vincing everyone I'm a lousy friend. Don't you believe him?"

Woodrow looked up at me with his big brown eyes. "I know you're a good friend," he said. "Harry's a good friend, too, but sometimes even best friends make mistakes. When that happens, I for-give and forget."

"Woodrow is right," Bubba interrupted. "Harry is a good friend. Before his humans left for vacation, he always shared his toys with me."

Woodrow nodded, dragging his long

ears through the grass. "Harry is lonely and confused. He's a little sad. He needs an extra pat or two this week, and he thinks telling stories will get him more attention. Sometimes telling *is* the right thing, but now he's carried away with tattling."

Woodrow had that right. Harry was definitely getting carried away, and his tattling was making my life miserable.

Could I ever forgive and forget that? Was friendship really worth it?

I didn't know what to do next, so I decided to do what Woodrow would've done in my situation. Take a nap.

I circled a nice shady spot three times, collapsed to the ground with a sigh, and closed my eyes tight. I hadn't been asleep long when something pounced on my tail. I jumped straight up, hitting my head on a bush. I swirled, ready to fight a tail-tugging monster.

ONE TALE TOO MANY

It wasn't a monster. It was Bubba.

"What are we going to do?" the little pup squealed. Bubba barked so fast that I could hardly understand what he was saying. I did make out "Harry" and "trouble" and "Sweetcakes."

"Oh, no," I barked, putting it all together. "Is Harry in trouble with Sweetcakes?"

Bubba nodded and hopped up and down in front of my nose like a bouncing ball. "Do something!"

Watching Bubba bounce made my

stomach tumble. "Settle down," I said, and put my paw on Bubba's head to stop him from moving. "Tell me what happened."

Bubba's tongue dropped out of the corner of his mouth. He licked his lips before telling me the scoop. "Harry tattled on Sweetcakes," Bubba panted. "He told everyone that Sweetcakes is a cheater—that's why she can do all the tricks so well. Now Sweetcakes is cornering Harry by the shed."

"A cheater?" I squealed. Harry had

finally told one tale too many. No one called Sweetcakes a cheater and lived to tell the tale. That was a Fido Fact.

I'm a warm-blooded hound, but my blood ran cold at the thought of Sweetcakes bullying Harry. Suddenly, it didn't matter that Harry had made me mad. All that mattered was that he was my friend, and he needed help.

"Tell Woodrow, Blondie, and Floyd that Harry needs their help," I told Bubba. "Then get Fred."

"You mean you want me to tattle?" Bubba asked.

"YES!" I howled. Bubba was wasting precious time while Harry's life was in danger.

"But you said being a tattletale is the worst thing to be," the little pup said.

"Sometimes you *have* to tell," I barked. "This is one of those times. Now, GO!" I howled the last word.

Bubba raced off, already barking for help. Until help arrived, it was up to Jack, the Wonder Dog to save his tattling friend.

I turned and faced the shed. The shadows were long, and I heard growling—it was time for a rescue!

THE UNTHINKABLE

My nails dug into the ground as I bolted for the shed in the back of the play yard.

It was just as Bubba had said. Harry cowered in Sweetcakes's long shadow. Sweetcakes was snarling so loudly at the little guy that she didn't hear me come up behind her. Neither did her sidekick, Clyde.

I braced my legs, ready for the worst. "Leave Harry alone," I snapped.

Sweetcakes turned so fast, a dust cloud twirled around her dirty paws. She

grinned, showing one yellow fang. "I would think you'd be on my side in this dogfight," she said. "After all, that little mutt has been telling stories about you, too."

"It'll rain doggie bones before I'll be on your side, Sweetcakes," I said, sounding much calmer than I really felt. "Now, step aside and let Harry go."

"Jack's right, let him go," came a voice from behind me.

I glanced over my shoulder. There stood Blondie, Woodrow, and Floyd with a ball in his mouth. Just knowing my friends were behind me made me feel ten times stronger.

"I don't think so," Sweetcakes said. "After all, this runt of a dog has been telling the other dogs that I cheat. Let's get this straight. I do not cheat. That makes Harry a liar."

"Yeah, yeah," Clyde repeated after Sweetcakes as usual. "Liar, liar."

Harry trembled, his forehead wrinkled, and his eyes peered up at Sweetcakes's muzzle.

My buddy Floyd took a huge step forward to stand beside me. I was impressed. Floyd was not known for brave acts. I knew it took every ounce of courage he had to say what he said next. He was a little hard to understand because of that ball in his mouth, but everyone heard him just the same. "It's unfair that you always know what Fred is

going to teach before we do," Floyd
said.

"That's true," Woodrow added, step-
ping in line beside Floyd. "You get to
practice with Fred at night and we don't.
So Harry isn't all wrong."

For a brief moment, Harry looked at
Woodrow, Floyd, and me with hope.

I nodded. Surely Sweetcakes would
listen to Woodrow. After all, Woodrow
was the voice of experience.

Experience didn't seem to matter to Sweetcakes. "I am not a cheater, and I will teach this runt of a dog a lesson for saying that I am," Sweetcakes howled.

Blondie took a trembling step forward and took a place next to Woodrow. "Then you'll have to fight us all," she said.

I looked at Blondie with new respect. She barely came up to Sweetcakes's chin, yet Blondie was willing to fight for her friend. Unfortunately, the truth of the matter was, we didn't stand a chance against Sweetcakes. None of us did.

I felt my heart beat three times faster. I could not let Sweetcakes hurt my friends. Stopping this dogfight was going to take drastic action. I did what I had to do.

"Sweetcakes is right," I blurted, figuring doggie bones would start falling from the sky at any moment.

"What?" my friends barked as all eyes turned to me. Even Sweetcakes and Clyde

looked at me with big eyes. No hound at Barkley's ever agreed with Sweetcakes, except for Clyde. I had just done the unthinkable.

Harry forgot he was scared and yapped louder than anyone. "Siding with her proves you aren't my friend!" he cried.

"I'm not taking sides," I said calmly. "Sweetcakes practices. That's not cheating. It may not be fair that she knows things before us, but it's not her fault."

The hair on the back of Sweetcakes's neck went down just a little. "I'm glad you finally got a brain in that head of yours," she told me. Then she turned back to Harry. "You're still not off the hook for telling lies about me," she growled.

My agreeing with Sweetcakes had slowed her down, but not long enough. She glared at Harry and took a step closer. Sweetcakes's mouth widened in a snarl, and slobber dripped from her yellow curved teeth.

"NO!" I howled.

FIDO FACT

Just then, Bubba skidded around the side of the shed. Fred was right on Bubba's heels, and Fred did not look happy.

"Sweetcakes!" he snapped.

Sweetcakes turned, caught by surprise, with her fangs dripping in a snarl.

"Sweetcakes, no!" Fred said, his voice very stern.

Sweetcakes whined, but of course, Fred did not understand her dog talk.

Fred took two giant steps and looped

his hand through Sweetcakes's collar. "Bad dog!" he said.

The rest of us gasped. Fred had said the two most dreaded words to Sweetcakes. But what Fred said next nearly made me bite my tongue.

Fred looked in Sweetcakes's eyes and frowned. "I'm sorry Sweetcakes, but I believe you need a few minutes to settle down. It's time-out for you."

"Time-out?" said Clyde whimpering. "Sweetcakes?"

None of us believed it, but that's exactly where Fred took Sweetcakes. Fred led Sweetcakes around the shed toward the time-out corner.

"You will pay for this," Sweetcakes warned as she walked past us. "All of you."

I couldn't worry about Sweetcakes just then. I hurried to Harry. Floyd, Woodrow, Bubba, and Blondie were right on my tail. "Harry, are you okay?" I asked.

"Thanks, Jack," Harry said with a nod, his black eyes peeking through shaggy white hair. "You saved me."

I shook my head. "Not just me, all your friends helped. Once Bubba told everyone you needed help, they raced to the rescue."

Bubba sat down and scratched his belly. "It's dog-awesome to tell when friends need help," he said, full of puppy wisdom.

"You mean, you'll be my friend again?" Harry asked.

"Of course," Blondie said.

"We never stopped being your friends," Woodrow added.

Harry's eyes looked a little watery. "I guess I've been a little lonely this week."

"I'm sorry I got mad," I said gently. "I should have said that we'd always be friends. So you don't have to tell stories to get our attention."

Harry looked down at my paws. "I'm sorry I tattled so much," he said. "If I had kept my big mouth shut, I wouldn't have caused everyone so much trouble. Can you forgive me?"

I grinned and remembered what Woodrow told me.

"Forgive what?" I said with a smile. "I've already forgotten, and that's a Fido Friendship Fact!"